DYLAN FECKER TOLD me on the phone, "A kids' library? What it sounds like to me is that you miss going out. He misses going out." I'm a writer, and Dylan is my agent. To him, a panicked social life is the sole bell-wether of mental health. In confusion he finds relief. Only his phone knows what he's scheduled to do next. Without it, he might starve, freeze, wander mistakenly onto public transportation.

"I go out all the time," I said. "The whole place is mostly out. Here, outside is the default. Indoors is shelter."

"When I say 'going out,' you know what I mean. And you miss it. Why can't you just say that? Why can't he just say what he means for once? Quicker and less confusingly? These are the big questions people want answers to. People are always waiting for him to say what he means, and then he says it, and Monte and I have to clarify." Monte is my editor.

"What do you tell them?"

"That it's all about getting to the center of the human heart. But you can thank me later. Are you writing? He's not writing."

"I would be."

"He's being smart. Don't be smart. I've tried calling you when you're really working: you can't wait to get rid of me. Lately you're lingering. Lately you want to talk."

"Oh, is that what you're getting?"

"Don't be smart, I said. You're not writing. I admit I made a big mis-take letting you move out there all by yourself. I said, he's a big boy. Was I wrong."

"You weren't wrong. I took my temperature this morning. Totally normal. Sent myself off to school, kicking and screaming."

"Ha ha ha. Listen. You went out there, you said you wanted quiet. I say OK, he needs to turn it down for a while. I understand. I saw how the last couple of years were going for you, for you and Rae. And that terrible business with Susannah. Ordinarily, I wouldn't rush you. But Monte is eager to see pages. They're tracking you. Where is he with it, is the gen-eral tenor of things."

Dylan had allowed his sense of romance to persuade him that there trees, and schools named after presidents and trailblazers. And points on the compass. It's good to get back to the essence of things and I can't think of anything more straightforwardly essential than one of the four cardinal directions. The slogan of this town should be 'Welcome, and Get Lost.' That's what I did."

She nodded, vaguely. "Thanks again," she said. I'd been living too long at the outskirts of things to flirt coherently. Having delivered this somewhat loony monologue, I turned and entered the library.

It was 10:58 when I slipped into the Youth Services Department, opting to sit on one of the little chairs with most of the other adults who had remained behind to listen, or to watch their children listen. One woman had a baby balanced on her lap, the fine hairs on the back of its head whorled delicately, like a fingerprint. Most of the kids sat on the carpet near the bronze bear. As always, one or two of them sat on the bear itself, which was posed on all fours, one forepaw extended as if it were batting at something or taking a step, its face cast in the sort of expression that, in the higher mammals, reminds us of how truly inscrutable animals really are. (I have encountered exactly one bear out here, coming across it unexpectedly as I was walking from my truck down an unpaved road toward a rocky stretch of shoreline known locally as 669 Beach, after the county highway that comes to an end there. As I backed away I thought about how impossible it was to know what was in its mind.)

Another reason I like Salteau: the complete sense of routine—not of self-celebration but of *working*. At a reading in New York the introductions always make you feel as if Thomas Mann, or even Gandhi, is about to take the podium. At such events we're always assured that literature is in good hands. Salteau's introduction consisted of a murky announcement over the PA system, as if canned peaches had just gone on sale in Aisle 5. Beginning in five minutes in the Youth Services Department. And caregivers please do not lose sight of your children. Salteau entered the room, then transformed himself from commuter to shaman, removing his baseball cap, his fleece-lined jacket, his scarf. He took off his glasses and polished them carefully.

have it just throw it around. No skin off their nose, I guess. They dream about having so much they can go around giving away Cadillacs like Elvis. Of course, everybody's *near* the money. Work at a McDonald's on a busy stretch of the interstate and you're right on top of ten, fifteen million a year. But not everybody sees it laying around in big piles like we do here, though. People who do, they think, hey—easy come, easy go, casino makes money like *that!*" He snapped his fingers, then began to count off on them: "They don't think about overhead. They don't think about the cost of insurance and security. Computer systems, custom-designed systems. Maintenance and repairs. They don't think about the salaries for the entertainment. The chef. Place like this has an executive chef. The golf pro, the tennis pro. They don't think about the comps. They don't think about the cost of training workers in the pit or in the cage—that's highly skilled work with very high turnover."

"This is you saying the story's made up."

"This is me saying that it's a daydream they stuck a name on, apparently. You sit in that cage all day long surrounded by fucking stacks of cash, pardon my french. Why not? It's like plucking one grape off the bunch at the greengrocer, right?"

"So it didn't happen."

"That would be a hell of a lot of money not to report stolen, wouldn't you agree, Kat?"

"I thought it was possible that a company transacting a lot of its business in cash might not want to call attention to its accounting practices."

"See, now *you* have that countinghouse view. Stacks of money. Bags of money. Must be something wrong with it." He laughed warmly and with easy contempt. "It's a very interesting thought, Kat. But our financials are on file with about eight zillion government and tribal authorities, though. We're audited by a Big Four firm. Manitou Sands and South Richmond both."

Kat gave a little back-to-the-drawing-board shrug. "Guess that answers my question." She popped a piece of tuna into her mouth and glanced at her watch. He hadn't come close to disproving her conjecture, some people probably knew or guessed but never said anything; it was all fine with her either way. Then she left school and entered the zone of adulthood, jarring-enough transition; instant intimacy sheared away and replaced by endless prolonged acquaintanceship, people asked what she did and where's the copier toner and have you seen that movie; she dyed her hair blond for eight months on a whim and so she was white, an olive-skinned white, maybe one of those Puerto Rican girls who smell of peroxide; then she dyed it back to her normal color and the guessing game began all over again—Asian? South Asian? North African?—but somewhere along the line the Indian had been washed away, and if the subject never came up, she wasn't going to raise it, wouldn't apologize for not having hair down to her ass or Sacheen Littlefeather braids, for not wearing denim and buckskin everything, for not being overtly spiritual, for not having huge gaudy enameled silver jewelry and beaded belts, for not cashing her welfare checks at the liquor store and for not having stood in line for free cheese.

"You went off the reservation, that's for sure," said Becky.

■ ■ ■

LATER, KAT SAT in the living room breathing hard. There was a good reason she wasn't in touch with Becky: it upset her. She thought about what had come out of her mouth, unsummoned: I ain't Mrs. Danhoff no more. When's the last time she used a construction like that? Was that "Indian"? Or just bad English? Or something else entirely?

PART 2

...

THE ETERNAL SILENCE
OF INFINITE SPACES

...

"What it is is a vandalizing, Dada riposte to commerce. You have to go to the *Times Book Review* if you want serious vandalism directed against art."

"Why aren't you more worried about this?"

"When they start speculating aloud whether if you chain forty million Shakespeares to forty million oranges will they eventually come up with the collected works of Darius the Chimp, I'll start worrying."

"Oh, so you'll let me worry about it. Terrific. Take a number. Monte will figure it out. Monte's job is to figure it out. Like this is what I signed on for, saving an industry. Listen, when I started, I just wanted to publish a few good books, have a few laughs. Nobody's laughing now. Not since the Germans bought us out. People are cringing in the hallways. They're puking in the toilet stalls before each meeting with sales. Editors who haven't worn a tie to work in twenty years are showing up in suits, as if that alone will placate our Teutonic overlords. The big decisions have already been made, though, I suspect. There are telling indications. But who can really say for sure? At three a.m. the e-mails start rolling in from Stuttgart. Strictly Kremlinology time. What does this mean? What does that mean? Shepard and I have these fierce, whispered conversations when sane people are supposed to be dancing their cares away at after-hours clubs. But I don't want to worry you. You have an entirely different job. How's my new book?"

"Hopelessly stalled."

"I just wanted to let you know that I have two pages reserved for you in the Fall catalog. They've dummied it up, and we didn't even *lorem ipsum* it. The pages just have 'AM3' across them. The long-awaited follow-up by AM3."

"It won't be ready for Fall."

"*Untitled Novel.*"

"Great."

"Hey, I'm counting on something from you, buddy. I believe that was our understanding. You were going to go out to Michigan and get to work. I was going to sit in New York and patiently wait. You were going to

"Yes."

Nables drew a breath. "I believe that I have earned a measure of respect from those with whom I work, Kat. To be clear: respect is not something that is doled out in accordance with mystical beliefs. One earns it. Respect needs to be earned. Beyond the basic conceptual framework of it as something of which we are all deserving, respect is not something we come to automatically, nor is it something we apportion equally. We do not put it on a scale and then cut it into wedges for equal distribution to all. Personally, I find respect to be a challenge. A true challenge, as stern a challenge as any my mother encouraged me to step up to as a young boy. How do I respect this person with whom I disagree? Who observes unfamiliar customs? Who simply looks different? How do I grant them the benefit of the doubt, which perhaps is all respect adds up to in the end? How do I find a way to do this?"

The large white flakes descended thickly, falling at a slight angle; decorous and individually distinct in the streetlamps, swarming and chaotic at the level of the headlights. They massed on the windshield between swipes of the wiper blade.

"Rising to this challenge has given me a certain ability to empathize, Kat. I mentioned subtext earlier. For any event in reality, there is a subtext that is equally real. Perhaps more real. Perhaps reality is nothing but subtext. Human beings offer up very little that can be trusted on the basis of appearances alone. One could argue that what we call reality often is no more than the setting in which subtext thrives. Look at us in our clothes. What are you wearing right now?"

"Excuse me?"

"Never mind that. I am suggesting only that beneath our outward appearance, things often are quite different, radically different, than what one might anticipate. I wear a sign that says 'Midwest Editor.' You wear a sign that says 'Staff Writer.' Do you understand what I'm trying to get at?"

"Not exactly."

"What I am trying to express is that the outward signs say that we are not equals. But inwardly, we are equals, in many respects. And therefore,

"I saw you taking notes. You don't have a kid with you."

"Not bad," she said.

"What paper?"

"Who says it's a newspaper? Maybe I'm a blogger."

"Ah. A blogger." He formed a cross with his index fingers and aimed it at her.

"Welcome to the digital frontier."

"No. You forget, I'm the one trying to escape."

"Then you'll be relieved. I'm strictly old media. The *Chicago Mirror*. I feel like I have to identify myself because my boss would not be amused for one second by my impersonating a blogger."

"Feels like his world is vanishing, huh?"

"It *is* vanishing. Blogs are like the good old days. It's Twitter we have to worry about now."

"What's 'Twitter'?"

"Never mind. Just aim that cross somewhere else."

"Long as you're not a blogger."

"When in doubt, blame the bloggers."

"It's all their fault."

"And so where's *your* kids?" she asked.

"Brooklyn."

"You mean like, *Brooklyn* Brooklyn."

"Over the famous bridge."

"I thought you seemed out of place."

"Back. In place, I mean. I'm from the midwest originally."

"Imagine that." Kat checked to see if the pictures were uploading. The guy muttered something; can't believe you found him or thought nobody would find him or something like that. She looked up sharply. "What?"

"I said, I guess Cherry City is about to lose John Salteau to the big time."

"You've got a funny idea what the big time wants."

"Oh, that's not true. I watch a lot of television. There's an endless

I like to do this sort of thing all at once. This here is your now and your then. How you get things done. Can't aim a gun and then come back and fire it later. My nana taught me that. Target won't wait. Sight won't just stay lined up with the target. Got to aim the gun and then squeeze the trigger if you intend to hit anything. Otherwise it's just a waste of time and ammunition. So while I reach you late, I been on the phone since six o'clock. Six Fellows per year each working through six-year terms means thirty-six Fellows total. Know something? Y'all usually pick up the phone. Can't say I'm surprised. People always pick up and talk to the money. Love can roll over to voice mail, but you're there for the money. Nana taught me that one, too. And y'all like to talk, I can say that. Chatty folks, you people. Like to chat my ear off, like as if I might take the money away from you if you don't explain yourselves. I honestly have to say that I would prefer it if the calls were quicker. Seven hours on the phone with the Boyd Fellows. Twelve dollars of Boyd Fellowship money per call, I reckon. That's two hours' wages for a hand on my ranch. Three hours if he's a Meskin. That's the price of the blue plate special at the Avalon Diner. That's the price of a à la carty car wash at the Fast Lube. Plus toll charges. Plus the not inconsiderable value of my own time. Seven hours chitchatting about physics and poetry and whatnot. I have to say, I don't know what I'm supposed to be trying to prove to myself. We have a network of respected nominators, a esteemed committee of selection, and a distinguished advisory board to guarantee a top-quality pool of candidates. And the Fellowships are famously offered without strings, although I was not a party to that particular decision. I have to say I would prefer it if there was a string or two. Doesn't matter how much someone likes rhubarb, they still got to pay for the pie and coffee. That's also Nana. Not much got past Nana. There's a whole bunch of reasons why I'm glad she's dead, but the biggest is that she didn't have to live to hear someone explain how they were writing a whole damn book talking about how whether Nathaniel Hawthorne was gay with Herman Melville. I just had that conversation. Shona Greenwald. Nice lady, but big as a cow. Got her fellowship couple years before you. Field of gender studies. Hawthorne and Melville sitting in a tree. New one fall for it. He's falling for it. He's got this labyrinth he forces himself to spend years working his way through, with this total enigma at the center, so of course he's thinking of it as an enduringly profound artifact that he's creating. It's just a fucking story, Sandy. That's what you writers always forget. Look: five million years ago some poor schmuck of a hominid was wending his way across the savanna when a lion jumps him and drags him off into the bushes. For millennia he's just a skull and a pile of bones buried beneath the mud until an anthropologist digs him up, dusts him off, and ships him to the British Museum. The guy never did anything except scratch himself, throw rocks, and eat grubs, but now he entertains, informs, and enlightens millions. How are you going to top that? Maybe in a couple of hundred years there'll be a few dozen doctoral dissertations on your work that no one's looked at in decades. Movies, Sandy: the closest you'll ever come to leaving your jawbone preserved in the mud somewhere in Africa will be the movies made from your books. They won't even be remembering your work. They'll be remembering fucking Ethan Hawke."

■ ■ ■

IT WAS GRIM-ENOUGH news, possibly unsurprising. The idea of being *in breach of contract* thrilled me a little, though. It even sounded vaguely prosperous, to have a contract it was possible to breach. Apart from ridiculing my seriousness, or what he misperceived as my seriousness, about my work, Dylan had actually sounded indignant on my behalf, as if he really believed that I needed only focus and a little more time. Well, he could fight it all the way to the gates of the old city of Stuttgart, but nothing could change the fact that I was not among the authors dawdling over their manuscripts, I was among the dreamers who wandered lost in a gauzy dream of famous achievement, puffed up by my own ego. I shook my head, knowing, finally, that there would be no book.

Drama of the book as the adversary. Drama of the book as the difficult offspring. All horseshit. The drama of the book was that it wasn't features, they all knew. It was pretty easy to persuade myself that I was someone important. Beyond the Palace of Versailles, though, things were different. Out there the big question was ingenuously poignant, and cutting: "Have they ever made a movie out of one of your books?"

In my case, as we have seen, the answer was yes—that random Hollywood Santa had visited my home and scattered largesse; enough of it, really, to inflame me with an unfamiliar greed; not a greed that would remain unfamiliar for very long, although I managed to coil all its malign energies once again, store them against the day when I could no longer delay my own gratification; coils that would come undone all of a sudden, undoing with them all those pragmatic habits, that smooth routine; *habits* and *routine* being the very things I'd confused for me, for myself, for who I actually was, when in fact *who I was* was a slavering maniac waiting for an opportunity to spring myself from self-control; a hungry, envious, vengeful, weak, and treacherous maniac, as well as a consummate bullshit artist; the first whiff of that bullshit arriving the moment I got my hands on that first check from my Hollywood agent; an ordinary blue-gray check imprinted with a number not all that big in the overall scheme of things, but sufficient, more than sufficient, to reveal all the potential for vulgarity I possessed.

That time, we'd thought of greed as a lapse, Rae and I. Dazzled, we thought it was understandable to mistake money for freedom. Who wouldn't? It is, in its way. It's better to have it than not to have it. Who doesn't believe that? *Pace* Count Tolstoy, but I can't make a case for becoming a wandering mendicant. I am a product of my century, the twentieth, that is, which can be said to have consisted of a sustained effort to repudiate History's Most Beloved Author. It is better to have it, as I prove each and every day here, in Michigan, free to drive my brand-new truck and wear my brand-new clothes, free to sit on my brand-new furniture and type on my brand-new computer, free to eat my brand-new food heated in brand-new pots and pans, all mounted in the midst of this brand-new life I rustled up for myself—Cherry City was a perfect setting for the expensive and flawless gem that reflected my unhappiness

"Becky. Anyway, the point is that malls are bad news. They make people feel terrible. People's relationship to shopping is at a low ebb. They get angry at the merchandise. This is bad. Retailers need specialized environments. Now, if you're selling dishwashers and Blu-Ray players, you open a big bare space made out of cinderblocks where every exposed beam is covered with spray fire retardant. This says, 'This ugly place makes you suffer a little; we'll try to make it as quick and painless as possible, but we're also going to make you *see* what goes into giving you your deep deep discount. But imagine how great your new dishwasher will look in your kitchen rather than in this hellish no-man's-land.' That one's easy. But if you sell books, what's the balance you need to strike, how do you make Malcolm Gladwell seem necessary while making him seem as frivolous and commitment-free as a popcorn movie at the same time? You don't want people weighing the relative merits of Malcolm Gladwell versus an Auntie Anne's pretzel. Things could get really ugly for Malcolm. And you definitely don't want people comparing the untapped utility of an unread Malcolm Gladwell book with the endlessly tapped utility of a fifty-five-inch HDTV."

Kat deadpanned, "Who's Malcolm Gladwell?"

Andrew Meisler shook his head, chuckling. "Who's Malcolm Gladwell. Do I like you or not?"

"You like me." Kat started on wine #4. He patted her thigh, then let his hand light on it. She let it remain there, feeling an oncoming attack of what Justin liked to call *acting out*.

"We don't call it a store," he continued. "We call it a *commons*. It's a template devised specifically for places like this, relatively sophisticated dots on the map that are miles from anything resembling a viable alternative to what we offer. We think of the commons as a place where an irresistible conversation is always happening. And there's only one way to be part of it."

"Buy something."

"That's a kind of reductive but basically accurate way of putting it."

"Lots of luck."

PART 4

...

SMARTBERRIES

...

bed, and was leaning back to lift her right leg to remove her boot. She repeated the act with the left boot, and then reclined, supporting herself on one elbow as she reached out to take the cup of wine from me. She drank, straightening her back and pushing out her breasts, then looked at me.

"OK?"

"OK." I gazed at her. "You know, I wasn't sure we were going to see each other again," I said. I tried to say it lightly, but my voice shuddered as I spoke.

"You knew we would."

"Yeah, no, you seemed equivocal."

"I'm a married woman, birdbrain."

I put my hands on her shoulders and pushed, lightly. She fell back, giggled.

"Why would I write him a note?" she said, returning to the subject. I put my hands on her thighs. "Or is it because I'm a journalist you figured I'd want to, what? Document it?" I straightened my fingers so that the heels of my hands and my thumbs were pressing against her thighs and then moved them slowly up and in. "Or because *you're* a writer? Write a note, explain everything." I put my fingertips on the thin band of flesh that had appeared between the waist of her jeans and the hem of her blouse, moved them up and under the blouse, felt smooth skin and the ridged swell of her rib cage. "It's like when someone commits suicide. They always ask did he leave a note." I moved my hands back out from under her blouse and placed them on either side of her torso, put one knee on the bed between her thighs, and leaned over her to kiss her. She grabbed me by the hair and pulled me toward her. For a few minutes it was all tumble and sprawl, friction of clothes against skin, seams twisting the wrong way and digging in, gasps and moans. It was different than it had been in the car—that had been tender and tentative. Here it was clear that a decision had been reached, that all second thoughts would be afterthoughts. I reared back and pulled off my sweater and turtleneck, then helped her remove the blouse. Beneath it she wore a red brassiere, and she sat up to unhook it. I pushed her back down. I wanted to sustain lined up on its top. Hanshaw opened one of them and discovered that it was empty inside.

Five minutes later he was back in his truck, persuaded that there was nothing to be discovered in Bobby's office. He was driving to pick up Jeramy, nominally his "cousin" but really just a footloose boy of uncertain pedigree who'd grown up within shouting distance. Hanshaw had, at various times, arrested three of the men who had, at various times, lived in Jeramy's house; all on drug charges and one on a domestic dispute call. Two of the drug offenders had been all right if too stupidly obvious in their habits living next door to a cop. The third man had been mean, slit-eyed and half-smart, and Hanshaw was pretty certain that he'd been responsible for the poisoning death of his dog, so in the course of arresting the man for choking Jeramy's mother he'd found a reason to break his jaw with the barrel of the Colt Python he used to wear when he was in uniform, a big, heavy, reliable gun that didn't look ridiculous strapped to his massive hip. After that Hanshaw hadn't been able to shake Jeramy, whose enthusiasm hadn't waned even after Hanshaw had had his own troubles and left the tribal force.

Jeramy's mother opened the door. She and Jeramy lived alone now.

"Hanshaw," she said. The house was one long dim hallway, with doorways poking out on either side.

Hanshaw crossed the threshold. "Is he here?" he asked.

"'Course he's here. Where's he going to be at? The library?"

"Maybe he's reading a book right now," said Hanshaw.

She laughed once, a sharp bark. He passed her and went through one of the doorways. It was cold in Jeramy's room. Jeramy was lying on the bed wearing a down jacket and a set of headphones. He was tall and thin, the stubble on his pale brown scalp mapping his already receding hairline. His eyes were closed.

"We have a job of work," said Hanshaw. He knew that the boy wouldn't be able to hear him, but this was a ritual he performed to satisfy his sense that the world had become ridiculously and unmanageably barbaric during his lifetime. He repeated himself, louder, and struck the boy

Hanshaw gave him five dollars and the kid opened the door and got out. He crossed the street with a practiced hobbling gait, as if he were wearing a set of leg irons. Hanshaw watched him go. He thought it would be unnameably righteous if the kid could walk in there amid all the hiss and steam, the pale young people composing poems and screenplays while some singer with a dorm-room-tragic voice played over the sound system, and swipe one of their fancy machines. In Hanshaw's youth the place had been a record shop; he remembered fondly the deep-space serenity of flipping through the bins at the rear of the store on yet another squandered afternoon. Five minutes later, Jeramy appeared in the street swinging a silver computer under one arm. He stepped off the curb and bounced on his toes until there was a break in the light traffic, then jogged over to the truck. He held up the laptop, displaying it exultantly, a goofy grin on his face.

TODAY

Mulligan leaned against the pickup, waiting while Kat called her friend. He had some questions. She paced, walking a serpentine path, occasionally glaring at a distant point overhead. The old man, Salteau, came out of his trailer, carrying something. He stood at the top of the steps and watched Kat for a moment. When he glanced Mulligan's way, Mulligan raised his hand in a wave. Salteau ignored him.

When she was finished, Kat walked briskly over and got in behind the wheel.

"She get her TV yet?"

"Still waiting. But I don't think she's going to be able to help with this."

"Help how? What does she have to do with this?"

"Forget it."

They rode in silence for a while. Mulligan discreetly worked away with his right pinky at the inside of his right nostril. Every now and then Kat would throw a quick angry glance in his direction.

"What?"

"He's gone."

THE FUGITIVES 271

a specific mutual enthusiasm—roller coasters—and decided that with their savings they would go on a single, extended pilgrimage to each of the tallest, steepest, fastest roller coasters in North America. They visited many rides, blogging about them and attracting enough of an online following that they were featured in several newspapers and interviewed on network television. Then, aboard the Iron Flyer at a theme park in Ohio one evening, the woman's lap bar sheared off as the car she was riding in began its descent from one of the ride's peaks: she had been straining against it, her arms upraised, screaming enthusiastically. She plunged more than one hundred feet, hitting a steel crossbeam on the way down, and was killed.

"I always wondered if the guy started smoking again after that," said Mulligan.

"Why would he?"

Mulligan was driving. A mist had settled low on the road, drifting and twisting in the headlights. Here and there were the eyes of deer, haunting the shoulders.

"I guess he wouldn't." Mulligan sounded slightly annoyed. "Life is so fragile, et cetera bla bla."

"So cynical. Suffer a loss, why not throw out everything else. Sounds familiar."

"Apart from the fact that I don't think smoking cigarettes is a total repudiation of life, I'm pretty sure I'm not the only one who's opted to hit reset."

"Well, that's not me," said Kat.

"Is that a fact?"

The speed limit dropped abruptly to thirty miles per hour. They were going sixty.

"They mean it," cautioned Kat. Mulligan braked and she watched the needle drop. A sign encrusted with the faded emblems of the Lions, the Kiwanis, the FFA, the K of C, the Rotarians appeared, welcoming them to Leatonville. Someone had blasted the sign with buckshot, and its lower left corner was pitted with holes. An intersection his friends' mothers had worked as domestics for Skokie Jews and Gold Coast Irish. His mother had been proud to be a secretary. Nables shook his head. No more. Now he had *assistants* and *interns,* young people who usually expected to be given something interesting to do. He spent time hiding from them.

He put on his jacket and left his file cabinet enclosure to ride the elevator to the eighth floor. The reception area there had been redone recently, walls knocked down, and now there was a chilly space to traverse, sparsely decorated with low-slung furniture, before he found himself standing before Melody, the receptionist, if that's still what you were allowed to call her. She didn't even greet him, simply picked up her phone when he appeared, spoke a few words into it, and shooed him with one hand toward Pat Foley's office.

Foley rose when he entered. Two other people were seated in the room. "Ike," he said.

"Hello, Patrick," said Nables.

"Ike, you know Susan Richter, our vice president of advertising sales. And this is Ted Denomie. Ted, this is Isaac Nables, one of our paper's crown jewels."

"Fan of your work," said Denomie.

"Thank you," said Nables. They shook hands.

"Ike, take a seat. Ted represents the Northwest Michigan Band of Chippewa Indians. He's on the board."

"It's actually the corporate commission. The business side of things," chuckled Denomie.

"Of course, of course," said Foley. "Ted's come to us with some concerns that Sue and I thought it would be worthwhile to bring you in on."

"What sort of concerns?" said Nables, carefully seating himself in a chair.

"Ted tells us that one of your people is looking into a loss that may have taken place at one of the casinos his group operates."

"Manitou Sands," said Denomie.

"That's correct," said Nables. "She's in the field gathering information.

natural life was I able to tell the difference. I fetched things, stood off to one side, carried money, beat people with my hands and feet when asked. I would have been happy to spend my life that way. Each day, the same as the last. There was nothing beyond Michigan and Bobby: nothing bigger, nothing waiting, nothing to come, nothing to catch up with me. So it seemed.

Yet the present is always the secret encampment of unintended consequences. Sedate as a neutered tomcat, it never occurred to me to *rue the day*, as the saying has it. Yet to rue the day doesn't begin to cover it. One would have to rue every day, every one that came before and every new one as it arrives and all those to come in anticipation. Only in death is there time to rue life as fully as life deserves. But I get ahead of myself.

■ ■ ■

OUR MONEY CAME from two streams. The original of the two was a laundry operation. Money from illegal sources was painstakingly changed into legal winnings. This took time, and patience, and it was not ideal, since the winnings were subject to taxation. Naturally, the government's lawful share was found, on the scale of dreams, to be disproportionate. Whose dreams? What dreams? Dreams of capital flowing unfettered, unimpeded, from its dreamy sources to the parched and dreamy basins it filled and brought to blossom. The everyday dreams of people everywhere. Does taxation ever find a place in those dreams? Does even the most liberal of minds, in its uninhibited moments, dream of higher taxes? These are rhetorical questions. And there were other, unofficial tariffs; doubtless you can easily imagine all the ways in which various officials were induced to turn a somewhat myopic eye to our activities. It was Bobby's job now to increase our margin. His solution was simple: he began to make money disappear during the minuscule interval when it has stopped existing. There is always an instant, as money changes hands, when it slips into limbo. It nearly always reappears, recognizable though slightly redefined—mostly in terms of whose property it has

44

I SPENT the next week recuperating. Locally, at least, the news dominated—a casino bigwig had been murdered, after all, and Argenziano's criminal record came to light, prompting a state investigation. I kept checking the *Mirror*'s website to see if anything had been written about it by Kat, but Chicago apparently saw no need to import news of violence and corruption all the way from northern Michigan. Kat ignored two e-mail messages I sent her.

No one associated "Alex Mulligan," a bit player and Cherry City resident several of the stories mentioned in passing, with the faintly scandalous author from New York, so I was left alone. Or so I thought, until I was contacted by the general counsel of the Boyd Foundation, who informed me that, at the instigation of an unnamed member of the board, he was initiating an inquiry into my personal conduct. As it turned out, the old Baptist sensibilities had not been completely purged from the